MOTH GIRL

VERSUS THE BATS

Michael Wombat

To Thea, for the music.

Introduction

This steampunky adventure with a flavour of thirties movie serials was inspired by a Twitter conversation I had with Thea Gilmore in early 2013 about anagrams, and then by her song "Start As We Mean To Go On". As the story progressed, other Thea songs lent their titles easily to the remaining three episodes, and more song titles found their way into the text. See how many you can spot.

The name '*Moth Girl*' came out of an anagram of Thea's name – in fact Ratporchrico's opening phrase in this story is that very anagram.

Do take the time to listen to Thea's splendid music. If you're not a fan already, you soon will be.

www.theagilmore.net

Contents

Start as we mean to go on

Out of the moonlight they sped in their thousands, swift as death, razor wings glittering in the pale glow of the Wolf Moon. In the frost-shrouded city below, the final toll of the curfew bell faded. Latecomers hurried inside, the hems of their capes whisked through narrowing gaps as doors were slammed, shutters bolted and chimneys blocked.

Those without homes huddled in hidden crevices, or burrowed under piles of rubbish as the bats hurtled out of the night sky. A high keening filled the air – whether emitted by the mechanical creatures themselves, or created by their sharp wings slicing the air no one knew – and suddenly the streets were filled with vicious whirling things, shredding anything soft that they happened across: clothing, flags, living flesh.

Here, a tunic accidentally left out on the washing line was shredded in seconds. There, a rat poked its whiskers out of a hole to investigate the noise and was seized upon by three of the deadly automatons. A beggar, too drunk on leafchew to ensure that he was entirely covered by the bridge under which he cowered, had first the shoe and then the flesh stripped from his foot almost before he could react. His screams brought more of the maniacal machines to him and he died quickly, his blood splashing the mossy stones of the bridge and darkening the stream that passed beneath it. Ten minutes later his bones glistened in the moonlight.

An anguished howl echoed across the town square as the bats found an unfortunate stray dog somewhere, to whom the curfew bell had meant nothing. Thea leaned on her iron spade and peered through a crack in the door. Her breath fogged in the freezing air. She rotated her arms, the better to sit the weight of her ankle length cloak on her shoulders. It clanked as it settled around her. Tonight's haul should be the last. The final collection that she needed.

She pulled the leather flying-helmet over her head, tucking her hair safely beneath the sturdy leather, and fastened the strap securely beneath her chin. She lowered the goggles over her eyes. The thick glass fogged for a moment and then cleared. Taking a deep breath of frozen air that shocked her lungs, she opened the door and stepped out into the maelstrom of wheeling metal.

Immediately the bats arrowed furiously at her, intent on slaughter. She heaved her weapon through the air in a scything arc, smashing several to the ground. Some struggled and rose again, while others sparked fitfully and lay spent on the ground. Numerous others flew past the spade, and threw themselves on her, tiny steel teeth and sharp claws tearing at the cloak. The air was filled with an almighty clattering as their tiny attacks bounced off the metal outer layer. A few attacked her head, but the old flying helmet, reinforced with chain-mail that Thea had sewn on herself, deflected the worst of the attack. She would have a hell of a headache later, mind.

She gasped as a bat slashed at her eye, but the goggles did their job, and she continued to gyrate strenuously, laying about her with the blade of the heavy spade, bringing more bats down around her feet. They flocked about her, trying their damnedest to get through to her skin, to rip her apart.

A sudden pain in her calf caused her to stumble. Damn. A bat had found one of the few remaining weak spots in the cloak. She felt its teeth, claws, whatever-the-hell sink into the soft flesh and tear through it. Quickly she switched the weight of the spade to her left hand, and groped down with her right to dislodge the attacker. She ripped it away painfully from her leg, and held it up in front of her. It squirmed in her gauntlet, pinpoint teeth, sharp claws and slashing wings flashing in the moonlight.

Thea tossed the metal horror up into the air and in one fluid movement swung the spade to bat it forcefully across the square. *That'll teach you, you evil little tin bastard.*

She continued swinging, gasping now and giving little moans as she tired. Her arms throbbed, burning with the effort, and the wound in her leg pulsed wetly. *One last effort, come on girl!*

She gave up on her to-and-fro sweeping, and simply circled wildly now, bats clanging against her spade as it cleaved the frozen air. Her head, her back and her arse stung from the constant battering from frantic metal attackers. She was becoming dizzy from the spinning, and decided to call it a day before she fell and allowed metal destroyers to creep under her protective shroud.

Slowing to a standstill, she waited for the briefest of moments for the world to stop spinning. In that moment she was attacked three times, and despite her dizziness threw herself frantically away, stumbling and rolling behind the huge bronze sculpture that dominated the north-east corner of the square, close by the ramshackle old hut that Thea called home.

Most of the townsfolk hated the giant metal skull, preferring the other bronze sculptures that dotted the town – the rhynocernose, the hellifaint, and an elegant wyvern with fully articulated wings that were driven by steam. The skull, glowering over the square from its cogwheel eyes, disturbed them, for it reminded them of their own mortality. Thea, as ever out of step with popular opinion, loved the skull, not least because on the hour, every hour, its cog-eyes rotated and it emitted a creaking groan the duration of which marked the o'clock. She especially liked it at this particular moment because of the cover it afforded her while she regained her wits and her balance.

A deep breath, then she scuttled quickly over the rough cobbles to her cottage, and banged rapidly three times with the spade handle on the door.

It immediately opened and she leapt inside, followed by half a dozen whirring bats. The door slammed behind her, and she concentrated on despatching those enemies that had entered with her.

Her grip now was tired, but Thea managed to smash five of the intruders to the ground before the spade twisted out of her weakened grasp and clattered to the floor. With a high buzz the remaining bat launched itself at her face, and she scrabbled desperately at it with her gauntlets, trying but failing to beat it off as it frantically scratched at her goggles. She felt a claw rake across her nose and cried out in despair. She was losing this one. One last desperate effort enabled her to fling it a foot away, but she was spent. Next attack it would get through.

THWOCK!

The bat flew across the room and smashed into the wall, propelled by a hard blow from a dark object. Small cogs and metal screws tinkled to the dusty floor.

"Ee, Moth Girl, they nearly got you there!" creaked an amused voice.

"I've told you not to call me that, Ratporchrico," Thea panted, shaking her head at the wizened old man by her side. He grinned a toothless grin, and put down the cricket bat he was holding.

"That's what you look like, though, out there in the moonlight with your cloak, your helmet and your goggley eyes. Like a giant glittery moth."

"I'll moth you, you old git, if you don't stop calling me that."

"You make no sense," he rasped good-naturedly, "How on earth do you *moth* someone? If you're going to indulge in badinage, at least try to make it coherent and quippy."

"It's badinage that I have to talk to you in the first place. How's that for quippy?"

"More pun than quip, but I'll allow it, given how well you did out there."

"Thank you," she nodded, "But they nearly had me. Now, shut your whiskery face and help me get this cloak off.

And then light a fire, for fuck's sake. I'm freezing my tits off here."

"Language, girl! You did not learn such speech from me. You're not too old for a slapped backside, you know."

"I'd like to see you try, old man!" she smiled, removing the helmet and shaking her burgundy hair free. It glowed in the flickering candlelight.

"You spend too much time down *The Murphy's Heart,*" Ratporchrico continued, reaching up to lower the heavy mantle from Thea's tired shoulders. "Common lot down that tavern, they are."

"They are good friends, too. Do not forget that. I'm going to whack some cayenne and honey on this wound. When you've got the fire going, pick up these bats here. I can start attaching these until them outside sod off. Then we'll gather the rest. I think I downed enough out there to fill all the gaps."

"So you reckon you'll have enough now?"

"You know, I really do. I put in a lot of effort out there."

"I saw," Ratporchrico nodded, "Moth Girl in thrilling action."

Thea shot him a glance, which he ignored.

"Tomorrow's the big adventure, then?"

She nodded. Ratporchrico peered at her closely.

"You're still sure? You're still determined to do this? To plunge into the unknown?"

"Somebody has to. It's been five full moons now, three nights each time, that those buggers have been coming. Tomorrow will make fifteen nights of terror for the people of this city. And what does Lord Liejacker do? Sod all. Oh, except hide. He doesn't even know why or whence they come."

Thea widened the ragged hole in her thick tights and washed the calf wound, then sprinkled cayenne to sterilise and stop the bleeding. Wincing, she smeared honey on top to aid the healing, and wound a strip of clean linen over the sticky mess as a rudimentary bandage.

"Well," Ratporchrico told her, lighting kindling in the fireplace with the candle, "My Lord Liejacker has decided that since his biplanes and his dirigibles are too slow to catch the bats, they simply cannot be caught. He's a great believer in the principle of ignore it and it will go away."

"I'm a great believer in the principle that he's a useless pillock."

"He is that. All that money he wasted on his portrait in feathers, and the ill–advised Sol Invictus Festival. And look at the idiotic way he treated the Baron a few months back for a simple sleight of protocol. Liejacker has not one iota of the sense or decency that his father had. His court—"

"Blah blah blah, yes. Will you stop wittering on about politics? We should concentrate on what we're doing."

The old man sighed, and stood up.

"There. Fire. Come and warm your tits while I gather these bats."

"Language, man!" Thea laughed at him. She sat on a rickety stool by the growing flames and warmed her boots, rubbing her hands together and flexing her fingers.

Ratporchrico carried Thea's cloak over to the large oak table by the back wall of the cottage and laid it out, metal side uppermost. He lit a second candle and stood it by the cloak. Finally he collected the fallen bats and put those on the table by the cloak.

"Ready when you are," he said.

Thea sighed and stood, tugging her tunic straight. She reluctantly left the warmth of the fire, and limped over to the table. She picked up one of the broken bats and worked the wings loose. She spat on them, and polished the metal to an unbroken gleam with a soft cloth. She sang as she worked.

Ratporchrico looked up from his book, a battered copy of *"So You Want to Pilot a Dirigible?"*, and a smile brightened his crinkled old face as Thea's voice soared above the continuing clatter and screeches from outside.

Thea took up needle and thread, and began to sew the bat wings onto the few remaining bare patches on her cloak.

This Is How You Find The Way

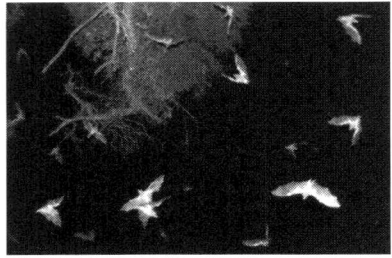

The following night Thea stood ready behind the cottage door, mantled in the heavy shining cloak, flying helmet and goggles snug on her head. She had a knife and a flintlock secure on her new belt, for who could predict what might shortly happen? Thea herself hadn't the faintest idea what to expect.

Outside, the deadly bats were still about their evil business, whirring and keening and destroying all in their path. Their usual hour of disappearance was near, however, and Thea stood ready.

Ratporchrico fussed about her cloak, checking each individual bat wing's newly fitted remote relay. One click of the big red button on the buckle of her belt should activate all of the cloak-wings at once. If that actually worked, if Ratporchio's intricate little switching mechanisms all functioned as they should, then one of two things should happen. Either the wings would gently lift Thea from the ground and take her with the rest of the bats back to whence they came, or she would be flung forcefully upwards to smash her head against the cottage ceiling. She devoutly hoped for the former.

"Bend your knees," the old man told her, and she complied, her boots creaking. He stretched and fiddled with the contraption attached to the back of her helmet. The "Automatic Blue" he called it, one of his many inventions. It was at heart a small boiler, perhaps two inches square. The tiny chimney attached would pump out a viscous blue vapour as she went, leaving a small yet visible trail that would linger for up to a day, so that she could find her way home again after... well, after what? Who knew what she'd find?

There might not even be a way for her *to* return, though Ratporchrico seemed fairly confident that since the bats were regularly able to find the town, there was a reasonable chance that Thea could discover that method at her destination and cause her cloak to do the same.

Ratporchrico patted her on the backside and she stood upright again. The Automatic Blue made a small *pocketa-pocketa* sound to show that it was working. The racket outside died down slightly. She let out a huge sigh. Nearly time.

"Ready, Moth Girl?" Ratporchrico asked.

"I've told you, don't—"

"READY?"

"Yes." She opened the door tentatively. The bats were milling about the square, circling aimlessly. They did not try to attack.

"Then it's time," Ratporchio told her, "Engage the bat wings, and just, you know, do your best."

"I will not disappoint you."

"I know. That would be impossible."

Thea smiled at him.

"Oh wait," he said.

"What?" she frowned. "Snag?"

"Did you have a wee? Best to go now. Who knows when you'll next get a chance?"

"Yes, yes, I've been, you disgusting wazzock."

"Then go, Moth Girl, and stay away from any naked flames."

Smirking, Thea pushed the red button.

Oh whoa.

What the f...

The cloak lifted around her and her feet left the floor. It was only bloody working! Wait, the doorway – how the hell was she going to get out of the doorway? She should have stepped outside *before* activating the wings. She waggled her feet frantically, which achieved absolutely nothing.

Ratporchrico sighed, and gave her a push in the small of the back. Thea floated serenely outside, then slowed to a steady hover, bobbing up and down slightly in the pre-dawn light. A splash of blood on the snow beneath her feet marked where a bat had torn her flesh the night before.

The Automatic Blue provided a small amount of thrust and in a spirit of experiment she leaned forwards a little. She began to move ahead, slowly, but steadily.

She was just experimenting with steering by lifting her arms to angle the cloak when she suddenly shot forwards, head first, legs trailing behind her. The breath was sucked from her lungs by the sudden speed. The bats were on the move, and they were taking her with them.

She sped upwards, and due south. Around her, the mechanical bats flickered their wings. Her grimace slowly relaxed as she realised that the plan, impossible as it had seemed, was actually working. She was following the bats back to wherever they originated, back to their cave.

Oh God, she was following the bats to their cave. They hadn't entirely thought this through, had they? For a start, how was she going to stop? She briefly considered hitting the red button again, until she noticed how high they had risen. The city below was tiny already. It turned beneath her feet as the bats curved to the right, eventually settling on a westward course.

Perhaps she could direct her own course a little. She angled her right arm up, clutching the hem of the cloak in her fist. She veered to the left. She lowered her arm and brought her direction back to that of her bat companions.

Success! In your face, Ratporchrico! The old fellow had been adamant that she would not be able to influence her direction of travel at all. He had thought the pull of the wings on her cloak would be too strong for her to divert. He had thought wrong.

She tilted herself to the right, beginning to enjoy herself. Her cloak brushed aside a few of the nearer bats, who simply ignored her and resumed their original flight plan.

Thea became more ambitious, she swooped and soared, turned and twisted, her breath vapour-trailing behind her to mingle with her faint blue lifeline. She laughed aloud at the unexpected joy of flight. She shouted with excitement. She imagined herself an angel, an avenging angel swooping to the rescue of her beleaguered city. The stars wheeled about her almost as if she controlled their arc through the heavens. This must be what it felt like to be an angel in the stars.

She devoutly hoped that she would be able to experience this glorious feeling again, once her mission was over. Her mission. Her thoughts were reluctantly dragged back to the task in hand. The ability to direct her flight, in addition to being a breath-taking experience, significantly improved her chances of dealing with whatever she found.

Now, when they reached their destination, she might be able to direct herself to a safe place. A shadowy hidden corner of the cave, perhaps.

She glanced around. Her tiny companions flew mindlessly on, rising still higher. The freezing air was getting thin, and Thea was grateful for the woollen gloves she wore beneath her gauntlets, and the extra set of underwear that Ratporchrico had insisted she wore.. The bat cave must be on the pinnacle of a high mountain, or perhaps even—

Wait, what was that ahead? Thea didn't dare release her grip on the cloak in order to clear her goggles, but through the misty glass it looked like an overly bright star. It was not Harpo's Ghost, that bright guide-star beloved of mariners and trans-desert caravans. There was Harpo's Ghost, over to the right, close by the fading face of the moon. And the dot of light ahead was growing bigger. Stars don't grow.

This object did grow. Or rather, she realised, it appeared to be increasing in size because it was getting nearer. Obviously, Thea reflected, clockwork bats do not roost in caves. Clockwork bats roost in... whatever the thing was that they were approaching.

It began to take on form as they closed the distance. It appeared to be vaguely wedge-shaped, with a protuberance at the point of the wedge. The sides appeared to be moving, rhythmically pulsing. As it came closer, Thea began to make out more details.

It was a mechanical behemoth, and now it filled her vision against the lightening arc of the sky. Huge pistons, driven by steam if the exhaust jets were anything to go by, pushed vast wheels around. These in turn acted via cogs and pulleys on great articulated sheets of metal that rose and fell in the roseate tint of the beginning dawn. At the rear of the flying machine, for such it was, a metal chimney of ornate design disgorged dark smoke. At the front, two large triangular satellite receptor dishes emerged like ears from a spherical cockpit, and below them a pair of large ocular windows allowed Thea to see figures moving about inside. This was plainly a craft of some sort. The whole contraption was a titanic mechanised creature of the skies. It was...

It was a colossal steam-driven bat.

Thea and her cloud of attendants were approaching the massive head. She hoped that the bats surrounding her, mere toys compared to the giant ahead but legion in number, would be enough to mask her approach from any sentinel that might peer out of the windowed eyes.

Behind her, the sun finally broke the curve of the horizon and threw blazing light on the craft ahead, which shone and dazzled like a fiery inferno.

Stay away from any naked flames, Moth Girl.

It was too late now for her to heed Ratporchrico's advice. She was headed straight for the bright flame of the mighty head.

She shook herself out of her fascinated torpor. It would be better if she could angle around to the side, maybe find a way to creep secretly into the body of the beast through the struts and cogs that worked the beating wings. She angled her cloak accordingly, but was rewarded with only the slightest of movements.

Damn. It had worked before. She tried leaning the other way, but was unable to affect her course significantly in either direction. Either the aerodynamics of the cloak were less effective in the gruel-thin air at this height, or the power of attraction between the mother ship and her minions was far stronger at this small distance.

Thea released her grip on the cloak entirely, leaving her hands free. It made no difference. The cloak, attached securely around her shoulders, continued to support and direct her. Wherever the bat cloud was going, she was going too. She briefly considered hitting the power button on her belt, but a glance to the shadowed earth, far far below, convinced her that stopping the wings would only lead to long cold fall and a certain death.

Perhaps the rising sun would blind any watchers ahead, and allow her to slip in unnoticed. It was difficult to make out much through the dazzling reflections, but she could not see anyone gazing out of the windows at her; just dim, blurry figures moving about. Another movement of darkness drew her look down.

Below the eyes of the Steam Bat, a dark crack appeared in the bright metal face. Slowly it widened. The maw of the beast was opening, hungry and black. Thea, enveloped in her glittering swarm of attendants, was flying directly into the mysterious darkness and into the belly of the beast.

Regardless

After the reflective brilliance of the outside, now she could see nothing. Her goggles steamed up in the warmth of the interior, and Thea pushed them up out of the way.

She could still not clearly see. Her pupils needed time to adjust, but did she have time? For all she knew she could be flying towards danger, capture, or both. Perhaps she should end her flight, but then could she be certain that there was actually a floor underneath her? Yes, she had flown into the mouth of the bat, but there was no guarantee that there was an internal base to the thing, or that if there was a base that it wasn't covered with, say, deadly spikes.

Finally her eyes began to clear. She began to make out a moving spiral shape in front of her.

Wait! The spiral was the movement of bats circling in to pass through a tiny hole just a few yards ahead. She was about to crash into the wall.

She frantically palmed the Big Red Button and fell, knocking several bats out of the way. They chittered and righted themselves, swerving back up to enter their hole in the wall.

Pain shattered through her shoulder as it hit the ground first, and she rolled onto her front. She tried to push to her feet, but her sense of balance seemed all wrong and she fell over once more. The heavy cloak wasn't helping, and she struggled to unfasten the strap that held it about her shoulders. She would need the cloak to return home, certainly, but that did not mean she could not take it off for the time being, at least until she found her feet.

Suddenly she realised that her sense of balance was not the problem. The floor itself was actually moving. It trundled past the walls at no more than a walking pace, but it was enough to throw her off her feet when unaware. She pushed herself to her knees, leaning against the movement of the floor. The cloak of wings flumped to the ground as she managed finally to unbuckle the clasp, and she immediately felt lighter and more capable. A quick rotation of her shoulder assured her that she had suffered nothing more than bruising.

She took a moment to take stock. She was kneeling on a sort of moving belt, made of a hard rubbery material, and stained with... well; she did not want to examine the stains too closely. The belt passed close between riveted walls of metal. Copper, judging by the warmth of colour. Expensive. Whoever had built this flying machine was rich. Very rich. As she watched, a plate passed by that declared, mysteriously, '29'.

Some ten feet above her head ran thick cables and pipes. The walls that she was passing between reached almost that high, but not quite. If she could reach the gap up there she might be able to climb out.

She looked behind to where she had fallen and realised that she must have been very lucky not to hit the piping above. Or had it been luck? She was now trapped in a channel with a moving floor.

She struggled to her feet and stretched her arms high. Her fingertips were at least two feet short of the lip of the copper barrier. It was unlikely that she would be able to jump high enough to reach, given the limited space she had to work with.

She tried it anyway, running along the channel against the movement of the belt and then leaping high and sideways. She clanged against the copper, but her fingers were tantalisingly short of the top.

She turned to try again, and saw just ahead the mouth of a wide pipe that opened above the channel. Before she could begin to consider whether this might be of any assistance the pipe emitted a gurgle, and a stream of filthy liquid shot out of the end. Thea was showered with a noisome mixture of detritus; brown slurry in which were mixed potato peelings, filthy oil, rags and bones, dead fish, old grounds of coffee and roses that had died a long time ago. Also some rather more disgusting things that Thea preferred not to think about. The stench was overwhelmingly disgusting, and she was so busy gagging that she almost missed the barred opening in the right-hand wall.

Almost. It was perhaps a foot square, with two diagonal bars running across it. She walked along the moving belt to maintain her position by the opening while she peered through. Under a light the colour of rust, colossal glistening pistons pumped, massive cogs turned against each other, and centrifugal governors whirled madly. Titanic forces were at work here. Machinery this large must generate enormous power. Such magnificent power, controlled and directed, surely could only be that which drove this airborne behemoth and kept it aloft. This must be the engine room.

Perhaps this small aperture might provide her with hand and foothold enough to climb out. Thea paused, allowing herself to move several feet from the opening, then ran back and leapt. She managed to insert her boot into the small opening, and with that brief support thrust upwards once more, getting a good handhold at the top of the partition.

Yes, she could get over this way. She began to haul herself up, then suddenly remembered her cloak. Damn. She'd better not lose that, if she hoped to see home again.

She dropped back down to the conveyer belt and ran along in the direction it was moving. It had carried her cloak some way while she had been trying to get over the wall. She was but a few feet from it when it dropped out of sight. It took her a second to realise that the belt ended here, doubling back underneath itself and dropping whatever it carried through a hole in the floor.

There was no way of telling how deep that hole might be, and she furiously back pedalled to avoid falling through herself. Her boots slithered on the slimy detritus that covered the belt and she tumbled onto her back. Frantically she rolled to her front and pushed with her feet. In utter frustration she felt her boots slide in the mess, and then she was kicking air as her legs reached the end of the belt.

She scrabbled with her hands as her waist reached the edge, her fingers unable to gain any traction. She felt her body weight begin to pull at her too as her backside swung down and with the final desperation of those drowning, clutched wildly for anything. With a frantic squeal she felt metal with her left hand and grabbed at it just as her body fell from the moving belt.

She swung from the left edge of the opening by one arm, the belt in front of her face continuing to throw rubbish below her. Luckily she had managed a good firm grip with her left hand, and she looked down, hoping to see a foothold or maybe even a ladder that she could use.

What she saw was the earth, thousands of feet below, bathed in the radiance of a morning sun. Her cloak, her one hope of returning home, was now a mere dot in the distance as it fell away to the distant earth. Still, that was the least of her worries. She searched wildly for anything that might help her to avoid following it.

In front of her face and just above the conveyer continued to dump rubbish into the atmosphere. There was no chance that she would be able to get a good grip there. An old teabag bounced off her chest as she looked to her right. The far side of the opening was not close enough to reach with her right hand. If she tried to swing over to it, there was a grave risk of her left hand losing its grip.

She dangled helplessly over the vertiginous void, her forearm beginning to ache now. Thank goodness for her gauntlets, which prevented the sharp metal cutting into her fingers. Without those she would already be plummeting through the clouds.

She looked up. There! Far up near the top of the copper wall was a large metal lever, about a foot long and tipped with an ornately wrought knob. The lever protruded from the bottom of a vertical slot in the wall, and a metal plate beside it declared, in a curlicue script, *'Maintenance'*. A smaller sign, equally intricate, told Thea that the lever was currently in the *'ON'* position.

She felt a glimmer of hope. She felt down to her belt with her free hand and unhooked her flintlock. It was a pepper-box with three barrels, so hitting the target first time was not vital, yet speed was important as her left arm was becoming weaker by the second. She took aim at the lever, adjusted for the weight of the barrels, and squeezed.

Close, but a miss, above and to the right of target. The pistol barrels rotated and she aimed once more, adjusting slightly left and down. This time the bullet hit the knob and the lever slowly lifted. Thank goodness for well-oiled machinery. The belt before her slowed and stopped. Now she stood a chance.

She was just re-attaching the flintlock to her belt when her left hand slipped. Just an inch, but enough to send a surge of alarm coursing through her. Now only her fingers held her from doom.

She drew her knife from its sheath and, hauling herself higher with the remaining strength in her left arm, plunged it horizontally into the hard rubber of the now stationary conveyer. It held, firmly. She paused for just a moment before hauling herself up and on to the conveyer, this time with the strength of both arms.

She needed a rest, but was worried that the lever above might fall back into the *'ON'* position. Investigating down the side of the conveyer belt revealed several drive belts and wires. Taking her knife she slashed at whatever she could cut.. Finally satisfied that the conveyer would no longer move, she collapsed onto her back. She lay there for some time, breathing heavily, heart-pounding, and muscles tingling with the release of tension.

"Sinew into steel, Thea," she told herself, and pushed upright. She walked back along the conveyer to the barred opening she had discovered earlier, and clambered up and over the copper wall with comparative ease.

Outside the copper walls that enclosed the conveyer belt, the noise from the mighty engine was much louder. Steam hissed, pistons shrieked, cogs squealed and governors rattled. Every minute or so there came an enormous resounding clang, as two vast yet unseen pieces of metal crashed against each other.

Thea threaded her way through the machinery, the red-ochre light glinting from the goggles atop her head. The engines produced a lot of heat, and she unfastened her helmet to take it off. Where the helmet had been her hair was plastered to her head by sweat, while the rest was wildly tangled where it had been flung about by her travails.

She dropped the helmet and goggles on the floor. Without the cloak she would not be flying back home and would no longer need them no matter what lay ahead.

She edged carefully around a large metal ball from which arcs of electricity reached into the darkness above. Then she stopped, puzzled by the thing in front of her. An enormous cylindrical flask, fully twenty feet high, stood in the middle of an open space. It reminded Thea of the ones, much smaller, that Ratporchrico used for his occasional experiments into alchemy.

This giant version was also made of glass, for she could see that it was half-filled with a liquid that looked deep-red, almost black, in the orange light that suffused the vast engine room. Three-quarters of the way up the flask a black line had been etched around the circumference, and labelled with carefully-crafted gothic lettering. It said 'ENOUGH'.

There was some sort of movement above the flask; a dark cloud that coiled and writhed. It gave an occasional flash of yellow light. Thea reached inside her waistcoat and withdrew a small spyglass that Ratporchrico had fashioned from cogs, pipes and old goggles. Holding it to her eye she was able to make out what the movement was.

Bats. Hundreds of metallic bats, whirling and spinning, their wings occasionally reflecting a flash of light. They emerged from a dark hole in the roof, and as each individual bat passed over the flask it deposited a small amount of matter before disappearing back up through the opening. As Thea watched, the stream of new bats slowed and eventually the remaining bats disappeared, their job done for now.

Were these the bats that had returned with her? And if so, what—

Oh God. It was blood. Blood and slivers of flesh and slices of bone that they had stripped from the creatures that they had killed in the town below. This horrific thought was mercifully interrupted by a deafening voice that reverberated through the engine room, louder even that the racket of the machinery.

"Well hello, my little train wreck," the voice boomed, "Welcome aboard the *Pipistrelle*, uninvited though you were. I regret that you felt the need to damage my property. Shame on you. However, you *have* managed to impress me. Twice, in fact."

"Wait!" Thea shrieked, irked that she'd been spotted. "Who are you? Why are you doing these things?"

"Your first impressive move was actually getting aboard," continued the voice, ignoring her questions. "Ingenious. You further impressed me by managing to evade plummeting to your doom from the waste disposal. Although now, annoyingly, I have to repair said waste disposal."

"Why are you collecting... is that blood? What kind of evil bastard does such a thing? And what does *'Enough'* mean?"

"I am certain that you have many questions to ask me, and let me assure you that I will be answering none of them. My autominions will be along shortly to repair the damage that you have done, and also, incidentally, to escort you back to the waste disposal hatch and throw you the hell off my vessel."

Something to Sing About

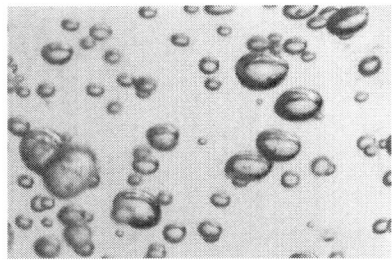 Thea moved quickly, ducking into a dark corner close by the sparking sphere. Her nemesis obviously had some way to see her; that much was plain. She lifted the spyglass once more and searched the vaulted roof.

The thick arched girders were spattered with all manner of bizarre devices, any of which could be a viewing machine. It was a waste of her time even to look.

As she put away the spyglass there came a loud bang from her right that was quite separate from the cacophonous rhythm of the engine. A door had opened, but a spout of steam from nearby obscured her vision for a moment.

"Can I help you?" scraped a tinny, scratchy voice. It sounded as if it came from one of those new-fangled wax cylinders.

Thea immediately dropped into a squat so that she could see below the hot cloud of steam. What she glimpsed appeared to be a grotesque amalgam of man, machine and arachnid. The uppermost part of the creature was more or less humanoid, though made of a metal that shone ochre in the strange light. The head moved from side to side, the arms were outstretched as if in welcome. On the metal chest was some sort of identification plate. It read *'29'*.

The lower half the creature was not at all human. The torso of the creature squatted on a circular disc of iron, from which depended eight thin articulated legs upon which the creature scuttled further into the room, its pointed feet tip-tapping on the metal deck.

"Can I help you?" it repeated, its jointed jaw falling and rising in a rough approximation of a human mouth. Thea stood and readied her flintlock. It turned towards her.

"Can I help you?" once more, as it raised a hand as if to beckon her forward. A curve of electrical energy streaked out of its fingers like a bolt of lightning. The air crackled and the energy singed the end of Thea's hair as it barely missed her head. The smell of burning hair mingled with the ozone tang of the electrical discharge.

Thea wasted no time. She raised her pistol and fired directly at the thing's head. The bullet ricocheted harmlessly off the metal skull.

Stupid, stupid, stupid. What did you think would happen? And why the hell didn't you reload?

She dropped to her knees as another bolt of crackling death passed close to her hip.

"Can I help you?" mocked the automaton, lowering its hand, its weapon, to point directly at her. She threw herself into a forward roll, moving immediately into a squat by the machine and scything her right leg across those spidery supports. The automaton crashed sideways, its legs waving helplessly in the air. Before it could push itself upright, she was on it and jabbing her knife into whatever orifice she could see.

"... help ..." the thing said, discharging electricity wildly from both hands in a vain attempt to throw off its attacker. Finally Thea jabbed the knife directly into the rectangular slot that passed for a mouth. There was a smell of burning and sparks shot out of the mouth hole as the autominion, as the voice had called it, became still and silent, save for the occasional sparking of a short circuit.

"Did you see that?" Thea yelled, still kneeling and looking up. "I'm coming for you, you freak, regardless of what you send at me! I'll be your silver bullet! I'll be your knotted rope! I will end this madness of yours, and I will end you!"

Silence. Of course, her enemy might have heard nothing of her melodramatic outburst, but at least it had served to boost her confidence, steadying her determination to overcome any obstacle in her path. She would prevail, no matter what dangers she met. Regardless.

"Can I help you?"

She whipped around to see a second autominion scuttle through the door, closely followed by a third. "Can I help you?"

It was like a weird scratchy echo, both automatons creaking the same inane words as they turned towards her.

"Can I help you?" "... help you?"

She thrust upward hard, leaping high into the air and somersaulting over an arc of lightning that would have taken off her head. She came down behind the nearest autominion, and whipping around, she took hold of both its arms from behind.

She forced the limbs together and directed the twin streams of electricity directly at its companion. The other automaton exploded loudly, shards of metal fizzing through the hot air, so that she had to use the robot she was holding as a shield. She wasted no time in leaning around and thrusting her knife into this one's mouth. It died like the first.

She ran to the door through which the autominions had emerged and found a corridor beyond. Tight-lipped with resolve she marched purposefully along it, boots ringing out on the deck. An autominion emerged from an alcove on her right. She thrust her knife directly into its mouth without breaking her stride, hearing it fall and spark behind her.

At the far end of the corridor was a metal ladder bolted to the wall, leading upwards. She gripped the knife in her teeth, dropped her gauntlets, and scaled the ladder; hand over hand, foot over foot.

She thought at first that she had emerged at the top of a high mountain peak. Before her stretched a jaw-dropping view, the arc of the earth's horizon far below, the ocean glittering beneath the bright sun like a sea of jewels. Glancing briefly away from the magnificent vista, she saw that she was in fact in a huge room, brightly lit by the sun streaming in through the huge picture window right in front of her. With a jolt she realised that she was looking out of the flying bat's eyes, which gave an unparalleled view ahead of the pteropine leviathan. No wonder she had been spotted approaching. She had been stupid to imagine otherwise.

"Hello, you wondrous thing. How *did* you get past my autominions?"

Thea turned to her right, towards the smooth voice that came from the shadows at the far end of the enormous span of glass. She flicked her eyes quickly about the large circular room. This must be the bridge of the vessel. Instruments and dials covered the walls, while in the centre lounged a plush chaise-longue, upholstered in what looked like a blood-red velvet. Beside it stood a metal pedestal into which were built lights, switches and levers.

The man at the far side of the window stepped forward into the light. He was tall, and wore a top hat that made him appear even taller. An embroidered frock-coat swept around his legs. The wry curve of his lips lifted his firm jaw pleasingly. His eyes flashed, or maybe that was just a reflection from the monocle, fashioned from a large cogwheel, fixed in his left eye. He leaned nonchalantly on a silver-topped cane.

"Baron Stonier!" Thea exclaimed.

"You know me? How flattering." He removed his hat and gave a small bow.

"But... you were banished," Thea pointed out.

"And yet here I am. It's almost as though I have no respect for authority, isn't it? Shocking, I know."

He closed the short distance between them, his gaze moving across her, lingering here and there, the smirk never leaving his attractive lips. He favoured his left leg, she noticed. The stylish cane was not just for show.

He gently took her hand in his and raised it to his lips. An unexpected picture of him kissing other parts of her drifted into Thea's mind. It was surprisingly difficult to dismiss the image. The Baron released her fingers and massaged his shoulder.

"Can you imagine why that might be?" he continued, his voice almost a caress, "Why I might despise Lord Liejacker? I was tortured, did you know that? Slow dislocation of one's joints tends to engender hate, I've found. But aye, I was indeed banished from the land. Not, however, from the air."

He frowned.

"I'm sorry; I have to ask—what on earth is going on with your hair?"

"What?" she shook herself out of her torpor and put her hands to her head. "Oh. Helmet hair." She smiled nervously and ruffled her dishevelled mane so that it hung more evenly.

"Oh, that's far better! You have deliciously lovely hair, my dear. It positively glows in this light."

Thea beamed. Her throat felt dry.

"Thank y— no wait!" What was she doing, engaging in chit-chat? This man was an evil mastermind, a heartless villain, not some fellow that she was trying to impress over a strong Bloody Mary down at *The Murphy's Heart*. "What the hell do you think you are doing?"

"Flirting?" he grinned. "How am I doing?"

God, his smile was lovely.

"Stop that! Stop... being nice. Just don't." He raised an amused eyebrow. Thea shook her head to clear her mind of the thought that had just crept in, of what Stonier might look like naked. She had to concentrate on the reason she was here. "I mean what are you doing with the bats and the killing and the huge vat full of gore?"

"Oh that," he answered dismissively, "Measuring my revenge. Drink?" He crossed to the pedestal and pressed a button. A door opened in the back wall revealing bottles and glasses which shimmered in the bright rays of the sun.

"What? No!"

"Oh, go on. Indulge yourself. After your exertions you must possess quite the thirst. If your intention is to attack me, then you will be fitter so to do without that tickle that I hear in your throat. If, after our little chat, you decide otherwise, then you and I will have had a refreshing drink together. Here, have a Berryade at least." He held out a tall glass in which ice chinked and a green liquid fizzed. Thea took it, noticing the Baron's slender fingers and manicured nails.

"Now, do please have a seat and rest those shapely legs," he indicated the chaise-longue. Thea saw little reason to refuse at this juncture. The Baron was right. After her recent exertions she needed a sit down and a drink, no matter what might happen next. She sighed as relief eased her tense calf muscles. The cool liquid coursed down her dry throat. It steadied her wheeling thoughts, too, and she finally realised what she had to do.

"A short time ago," she said, "You were planning to fling me out of the waste disposal."

"That was before I properly saw you," said Stonier, pacing before the vast window, nothing but a silhouette against the bright sun. "It would have been a shameful waste of a capable and intelligent, not to mention sexy, woman. Now, after meeting you, I hope that I can persuade you of the rightness of my cause. Perhaps you might even consider joining me."

"You can... sexy? Really?" Thea shook her head. "No! Piss right off. For all your handsome manners and charming smile you are still an evil blackguard."

"Charming? So, you accept that there is a chance you may yet be charmed?"

"Oh you have style, I'm quite sure that you know that. Yes, and a way with words, but your hands are also soaked with blood that cannot be hidden by with a likeable manner. At heart you are nothing more than a malevolent mastermind."

"Oh, come on. Being a malevolent mastermind, as you melodramatically call it, is fun! You'd enjoy it. You could say *Mwahaha*. And certainly you'd be the cutest villain I've ever seen."

"Look, I understand that you were badly treated, I do! What was done to you was wicked. But you cannot revenge yourself on Lord Liejacker by slaughtering innocent people and measuring your revenge in the number of lives you take."

"Of course I can. I'm doing it. And they are such little lives. *His* people, tiny and insignificant."

"No one is insignificant."

"They are, to me. Why should I care about their lives? They did not care for mine. When I was naked in Liejacker's dungeon, screaming my lungs out, not one of those innocent people thought to help me, or to object. To even tell that bastard that what he was doing was wrong."

"No-one kn—"

"Now I come to think of it, you did not object either." Stonier's eyes narrowed, and his smile disappeared.

"Oh dear, I fear I may have been blinded by a pretty face. For all your charms, though, you are as guilty as that lot down there. Worse, actually, since not only did you ignore the wrongs that were visited upon me, but you also now have the nerve to come uninvited into my domain and lecture me on morality." The smile was gone, replaced by a snarl. "You self-righteous bitch; you smug, sanctimonious whore! You think you have the right to interfere with my work because of your pathetically misguided moral concerns?"

"Yes! I mean no, my concerns are *not* misguided. The people you have slaughtered did nothing to you! You are so very wrong in this. You are wrong, you are evil, and you have one hell of a high opinion of yourself. You have to stop this."

"I've barely even started," Stonier growled. He stepped back to the wall and lifted a silver lever. A circular hatch in the ceiling irised open and bats tumbled out in scores, glinting in the yellow light that flooded the bridge. They arrowed at Thea.

She threw herself from the chaise-longue to avoid the vanguard as they sliced at her head, chittering. She caught a glimpse of Stonier, hands on hips, shaking his head at her and smiling. A bat cut painfully at her buttocks and she threw herself over onto her back, whirling her arms and legs as fast as she could, swatting away the bats that were trying to reach her. One got through and took away a chunk of cloth from her tunic. Another slashed the flesh of her cheek.

She began to feel dizzy as more bats broke through her desperate defence and cut into her clothing and her flesh. She could not last long, that was plain. Punching away a bat that took the skin from her knuckles, she threw a despairing look at the mocking Baron Stonier, just as the huge window beside him exploded into the bridge, shattered by the long, pointed prow of a red and yellow dirigible that had ploughed into the face of the *Pipistrelle*, its approach hidden by the glare of the sun.

Glass flew into the room, shards cascading across the bridge, glittering among the wheeling bats. The Baron was knocked to the floor. Thea felt dozens of small stings as tiny glass splinters cut her exposed skin. Before she could properly grasp what was happening, a small figure leapt from a hatch in the front of the attacking vessel, ran along the prow and sprang onto the bridge. Ratporchrico, for it was he, looked about quickly and grinned when he spied Thea. In his hands he gripped the end of a flexible tube that ran through the shattered window back to the dirigible.

Baron Stonier, sprawled on the floor close by, mouthed a foul curse and pulled the silver handle of his cane, drawing out a thin, rapier-pointed sword. Before Thea could shout a warning, he plunged the blade deep into the old man's body.

Ratporchrico grimaced and fell to his knees, but managed to turn a small wheel attached to his hose. An emerald fluid gushed from the end and drenched Baron Stonier where he sat on the ground.

The bats attacking Thea suddenly swerved away and swarmed at the Baron. She warily lowered her slashed arms and legs and turned to watch, horrified yet fascinated, as the deadly bats tore at their creator's screaming figure.

"Moth Girl!" called Ratporchrico, labouring to turn off the flow of green liquid from the hose. Thea struggled to her knees and crawled over to the old man while the bats bit and sliced at the thrashing, heaving body of the Baron.

"I told you—"

"Shu—HUU!" Ratporchrico coughed, blood spraying from between his wrinkled lips. He clutched his pierced side. Crimson oozed from between his fingers. "Throw the... the switch." He raised his hand in the direction of the silver lever on the wall.

Thea struggled to her feet and limped anxiously around the mass of bats clattering about the Baron, who had now fallen still. She pulled the silver lever back down.

The bats immediately left Stonier and sped back into their hole in the roof, which spiralled to a close after the last one disappeared. What they left behind was an oozing mess of bone, flesh and ragged bits of cloth. A cog-monocle lay in the spreading pool of blood on the floor.

Thea returned to Ratporchico, who now lay on his back, gasping for breath. She knelt by him and took his hand.

"Take it easy, you old git. Let's see what we can do about patching you up."

"It was the green... fluid. Attracts the bats... you see. He had gall... gallons of it hidden about the town. In the statues... the bronzes. He was... feeding it into the water supply. He had—"

"Ssssh, save your breath. I'll fetch cayenne, and honey."

"No use. I'm a bit too broken for med... brought some of the stuff... with me. From the skull... the bronze sku... thought it mi... might help."

Thea soothed a hand over his sweating forehead. "Shhhh, don't speak," she soothed.

"Bugger off," coughed the old man, spilling more blood. "I saw... through the spyglass... he had you drinking it. The green stuff. Had to... act fast."

"By crashing your ship into us? You mad bastard." Her eyes softened. "You saved me, old man. Thank you." She kissed his forehead. His eyes were turning milky. Blood bubbled down his chin.

"I think I broke the dirigible... when I... crashed it. Sorry." He looked up at her. "I'm a bit poorly, aren't I, love?"

She nodded. "Yes." Tears rimmed her emerald eyes and ran down her face, stinging a score of small cuts.

"Ah well. It's been... a good life. A long one. I love you, Moth Girl. I'm proud... of you."

"Don't call me that."

"Cheer up, girl. I may be dancing on the line... but there are still some things to sing about. We beat... the bad guy. Sing for me, Moth Girl. Sing me on my way."

Thea sniffed back her streaming tears and squeezed Ratporchrico's hand as he closed his eyes. His breathing was shallow now. Hesitantly she began to sing, her voice wavering and weak. She sang of hope and love and ascension and willow trees. She desperately hoped that her song gave the dying man some comfort.

Ratporchrico gave a rattled gasp and his grip loosened. He fell limp. He was gone.

Thea hugged his body to hers and threw her head back in an anguished howl. Great racking sobs shook her body. Grief overwhelmed her. What was she to do now? She felt abandoned, utterly lost, and thoroughly alone.

"Can I help you?"

An autominion scuttled towards her across the bridge, its thin legs scattering shards of broken glass. She began to reach for her knife. She paused. What was her life to her now? Continuing her existence was no longer important. She left the knife where it was and awaited oblivion.

The autominion came close, the '29' on its chest plate glittering in the radiance of the sun. It raised its hands. Thea closed her eyes... and felt something gently begin to soothe the cuts on her forehead. She smelled antiseptic, and opened her eyes once more. The metallic creature was bathing her wounds with a damp cloth. Thea frowned, totally confused by this latest twist in a day full of them.

Why the change from deadly spiderbot to caring mechanurse? Whatever the cause was, she suddenly realised that was glad of it, and was relieved that this was not, after all, to be her end. She released a huge sigh.

"Can I help you?" squawked the autominion.

"Can you help *him*?"

"I am sorry. I do not understand. Please rephrase your question."

"Can you help this man here?"

The autominion laid a hand on Ratporchrico's chest and Thea held her breath, hoping beyond hope.

"No. This man here is dead. Can I help you?"

"Help me to stand up," she sighed.

The autominion scurried behind Thea and lifted her to her feet. She limped over to the chaise-longue and sat down, letting its cushioned seat relieve her aching backside. She eyed the control pedestal curiously.

"Autominion?"

"My name is Stephen, Baron."

"Oh. Really, Stephen? OK. Well then, Stephen, do not call me Baron. Call me Th..." she paused. "Call me Moth Girl."

"Very well, Moth Girl. Can I help you?"

"Are you strong enough to push that dirigible out of the window?"

"Please define *dirigible*."

"The great thing there, sticking its prow into this vessel. Can you get rid of it, Stephen?"

"Yes, Moth Girl."

As she watched Stephen heave the wrecked dirigible away from the flying bat, Thea mused on the possibilities ahead of her. With a little cosmetic structural work, a few sheets of metal, several thousand rivets, and a few strong autominions, she was sure that the *Pipistrelle* could be altered sufficiently to look more like a moth than a bat. It would need renaming, of course. She rather liked the sound of *Luna*.

Her way ahead now clear, hair dancing in the wind that breezed through the shattered window, Moth Girl tilted the steering lever slightly to the left and followed the faint blue trail that led to home. First she had a funeral to arrange, but then... she smiled at the possibilities.

A loudspeaker above her head crackled into life.

"NS13 calling NS29. Serotine to Pipistrelle. Do you read me? Hello, Pipistrelle?"

Moth Girl will return in the thrilling adventure *"Moth Girl versus The Steam Scorpions"* in 2014

About the Author

Michael Wombat is a Yorkshireman living in the rural green hills of Lancashire with his wife and two adult daughters, who are all far more talented than he.

He has a penchant for good single-malts, inept football teams, big daft dogs and the diary of Mr. Samuel Pepys.

In his time he has been forester, bus conductor, busker and computer whizz-kid. He is very old indeed and likes to pretend that he takes good photographs.

Contact Michael Wombat

Got any questions? Or maybe you just want to chat me up? Please do get in touch. I'm on Twitter almost constantly when not writing, but you can use any of the other methods if you prefer.

Twitter	@wombat37
Facebook	http://www.facebook.com/wombatauthor
Photography	http://wombat37.wordpress.com/
Personal blog	http://cubicscats.wordpress.com/

Also by Michael Wombat

WARREN PEACE

A book for older children and adults, available in paperback, Kindle and ePub formats from Lulu, Amazon, Barnes & Noble and iTunes.

Influenced more by Seven Samurai, Zulu and Joss Whedon than by Watership Down, Warren Peace is about a young, nervous rabbit with an easy life – easy, that is, until the foxes come. With the lives of his friends and family in danger, Cuetip must undertake a perilous journey out into the big world to find help. On the way, he also finds terror, laughter, sadness, friendship, humans, cats, gods and perhaps most important of all, courage.

A novel about talking animals, but definitely not for tiny children, *"Warren Peace"* will grab both your heart and your funny bone and shake them silly.

Read the opening chapter on Page 49.

FOG

Definitely not for children, this one. Fog is an adult thriller available in paperback, Kindle and ePub formats from Lulu, Amazon, Barnes & Noble and iTunes.

You know how it is. We've all experienced it while driving. You suddenly realise that you have no idea where you are, or what your destination is. After a few seconds light dawns and you remember where you are going. But what if light didn't dawn? What if you continued to know nothing before that moment? You have no idea where you are, who you are, or why a bunch of nutters is trying to kill you. The only thing you know is that you have to run for your life...

Sexy, funny, violent and thrilling, Fog is not so much a Whodunnit as a Whatthehellsgoingon.

Read the opening chapter on page 58.

"Very clever. Funny and genuinely shocking at times."
"A joy to read. A rattling good yarn."
"A pretty damned amazing ride."

Cubic Scats

A gathering of rib-provoking and thought-tickling posts from the many blogs of Michael Wombat, available in paperback from Lulu and Amazon. Coming to Kindle and ePub soon..

Featuring a skeuomorphic cover by thrusting young designer Thom White, this smorgasbord of northcentric nonsense and recipes includes musings, Oliver Cromwell's head, fiction, a ghost chicken, oddities, history, a bone-eating snot-flower worm, dreams and yes, recipes. Amazingly, Wombie has also managed to pack over 300 photographs into this little book (and reader, beware: in one he is as naked as if he had no clothes on at all). Why read all these remarkable articles for free on the internet when you can buy them all in this handy, easy-to-read-on-the-bog format? Buy this and save yourself hours of Googling.

Read a sample chapter on page 64.

"A perfect read for the beach. Or train journeys." - Alex Brightsmith, about another book.
"Don't drag me into this." - Dawne le Goode
"Where did you put the bread knife?" - Mrs. Wombat

Warren Peace opening chapter

Snarling yellow teeth grazed Cuetip's rear end, but he somehow found enough extra strength for a mighty thrust of his back legs, and lost no more than a clump of fur.

The young rabbit zigzagged frantically as he sprinted, but his pursuer kept doggedly on his tail. Cuetip's heart pounded, his breath rasped, and fear pulsed through his entire body. He veered sharply around a bush, claws digging deep furrows into the hot, dry earth. The fox, vicious and predatory, would not be shaken off and followed closely, snapping at his backside. Cuetip had tried everything he knew to escape, but the fox had stuck with him throughout. The muscles in his legs and back were screaming in agony, and soon he would be too exhausted to run any more. Everything would be over – death in the sun.

If only he could find an entrance - a dark, welcoming sanctuary on the sun-bright hillside. He was sure that there was a burrow around here somewhere, if only the juggernaut of death behind him would give him a few seconds respite in which to get his bearings. The fox wasn't about to give him any quarter, however, and it growled with savage triumph as it made a swipe at his back legs with an outstretched paw.

Cuetip went tumbling over the short, dry grass, the blazing sun blinding him as it flashed across his vision, a cloud of dust rising up around him as he struggled frenetically to regain his feet. His mind raced, and he thought longingly of the peaceful calm that had been his just a few minutes ago.

* * *

The sky was a deep blue from horizon to horizon, broken only by the fiercely hot sun. Cuetip had nibbled off a blade of the short dry grass, pulled a face, and looked around for a dandelion leaf. He lazily swivelled his ears, searching half-heartedly for any untoward sounds. As always, he heard only the liquid trill of a lark somewhere in the blue above and the occasional *tick* as a gorse bush reacted to the heat. A bee buzzed fatly nearby. All was well.

Much of his extended family were scattered about the hillside, enjoying the warmth of the afternoon. Like him, most were feeding, but one or two of the more nervous youngsters squatted uneasily in the shade of the bushes, not daring to venture too far from a bolt hole.

Old Grizz, the most senior member of the warren at Farmend Field, sat upright near the top of the bank, head turning this way and that as he kept watch on his charges. Grizz was a bit past it these days, thought Cuetip, but it made the old rabbit feel useful to have the lookout's job. Besides, no one else wanted to do it. After all, they were safe enough here.

The twisting burrows and chambers of the warren undermined Farmend Field, a steep, roughly rectangular slope, south facing so that it caught the sun. A long time ago it had borne crops, but these days it was covered with rough grass and gorse. Along the top, northern edge of this incline stretched smooth, flat rock and rounded boulders and, beyond a short stretch of rocky ground, the scree-covered slopes of a towering hill. In theory, a single lookout on the ridge of Farmend Field could see all around, and give plenty of warning to retreat underground if need be.

To the west squatted a long-abandoned farm, the stone walls overgrown and crumbling, rusty machinery nestling in the nettles. The eastern boundary dropped sharply in a flinty cliff onto a tumble of rocks, and on the fourth side, at the foot of the slope, was their water supply – a sparkling beck that danced swiftly over smooth pebbles.

True, this meant that they could not burrow too deeply at the lower reaches of the slope for fear of flooding, but there was plenty of space under the higher reaches for all their needs. The rock on the North side extended deep below the surface, preventing them from extending the warren laterally, but Farmend Field itself was large enough to accommodate the whole warren comfortably. This was an ideal home for the rabbits, comfortable and safe. Had been for years. There had been no sign of danger for as long as anyone could remember, save Grizz. And yet the old male, ostensibly their leader, had insisted that they continue to keep watch.

"Don't know you're born, you young 'uns" he'd grumbled, earlier that morning. "In my day we were allus being chased by dogs and shot at by big two-legs folk. Kept us fit. Had to be keen-eyed. Had to be swift and watchful. AND keen-eyed."

"You said that already, Grampy" tiny Lucien had grumbled.

"Bah! Danger'll come again one day, you mark my words, youngster. That's why we've got to keep our eyes sharp! Pah! We should be doing more, much more, but you're all too lazy these days!"

"What more should we be doing?" Ernestine had asked, humouring the old rabbit. Ernestine, the second oldest rabbit in the warren, was sensible, sociable, and well respected by most.

"Lots of things!" gruffed Grizz, "Lookouts on all entrances, for one! Stocking up on food for another - them larders are pathetically low, you know! And we should have trained messengers for fast communication! We should make more designated latrines inside the warren, in case we can't get out! So many things we ought to do! And you lot – you lot just laze about, eating! In my day we had efficient defences, we knew how best to look after ourselves! Hrmph. In my day!"

Rant over, Grizz had subsided into a low grumble.

"In your day, were you ever chased by a dinosaur, Great Grandad Grizz?" young Lily had asked innocently, bringing a round of laughter from those in earshot.

After Grizz had tramped grumpily up to his lookout post, Ernestine and Cuetip had shared an amused smile as Lily had scampered by, chasing her brother Lucien. The twins had been laughing at a game of their own devising. The pair had been born recently to Ernestine's sister Twitch, and were not long out of the nursery burrow. Lily and Lucien looked exactly alike – dark-furred with pale rumps - except for the tip of Lucien's left ear, which always flopped down.

"Now, watch it you two!" Ernestine had warned, "Careful you don't fall into a gorse! I don't want to be licking any wounds tonight!" Then she had added, in that strange way of Aunties everywhere, "And don't come running to me if you break a leg!"

"OK, Auntie! Ooof!" Lucien had gasped as his sister bowled into him and knocked him rolling and giggling through the grass. They had scampered off down towards the stream, shouting a squeaky "Bye!" to Ernestine and Cuetip.

"B- B- Bye!" Cuetip had piped, cheerfully, but before he'd got it out the twins had gone.

Cuetip knew that he was a bit of a mystery to most of the rabbits of the warren. He spent a lot of time on his own, and no-one could work out whether that was because he was embarrassed at the way he spoke, or whether his stammer was as a result of his solitude and the fact that he didn't get much practice at talking. Oh, he was friendly enough - polite and civil to all - but he did not have any really close friends. Some of the less-polite rabbits made frequent fun of his impediment, and if any of the others ever thought about him at all, they simply assumed that he liked his own company. The only rabbit he seemed at ease with was Ernestine.

Cuetip had noticed that she had turned her gaze from the happy youngsters as they vanished over a rise, and was watching Hobb trying to clean his tail. As he had bent to the task, the big young male kept losing his balance and falling over backwards. After a couple of failed attempts, others would have found a handy rock to support their backside, but this did not occur to Hobb. He just kept right on reaching for his nether regions and toppling into a heap, convinced that if he just kept on trying, his sheer persistence would lead eventually to success. He was not the brightest of rabbits.

Ernestine, however, did not care that Hobb was something of a pea-brain. She admired him for his straightforward simplicity, his undoubted strength, and his loyal friendship. He was, in fact, her favourite friend.

Close to Hobb, a sneer on her unattractive face, sat Fluffers, Ernestine's (and indeed, Cuetip's) *least* favourite. She had been in conversation with Heather, a friendly little soul, who hadn't looked too happy to be talking to Fluffers.

"Perhaps I'll wander over there in a while and rescue poor Heather" Ernestine had commented.

"G- good th- thinking" Cuetip had managed.

He had glanced back up the hill, idly wondering whether old Grizz had remembered to eat anything, but the grassy lookout knoll was empty.

"Er- Ernestine?" he had begun.

"Where's the daft old idiot gone now?" she had muttered, following his gaze. The forgetful old thing had probably dozed off again, or imagined some tasty clover among the boulders behind him and wandered off after it. She had started to hop lazily up towards the lookout knoll to call him back.

A sudden movement from one of the bushes flanking the vacant lookout post had startled them both, and a dark, round object had tumbled down the hill. It had bounced twice on the coarse grass, before coming to a stop by their feet.

Cuetip could not focus on it at first. Then he had felt a chilling shock, as if he had been plunged into icy water, as he had recognised two blank white eyes staring at him out of

Grizz's severed head, bloody and tattered at the neck where it had been torn from his body.

They had both recoiled with fear as a shadow passed over them. They had turned quickly, Cuetip gasping, but saw with relief that it was only Hobb.

"Hi Ernie! Hi Cuetip!" he had boomed, unaware of anything wrong. He had looked down at the object in the grass. "Hi Grizz!" His smile had faded as realisation dawned, and horror twisted his features. He'd looked at Ernestine, hoping that she could bring some understanding of what he was seeing.

Ernestine, though, had had no opportunity to comfort her friend. A movement at the edge of her vision had made her turn her head, and look again up the slope. Two sleek red forms were swiftly moving down towards them, weaving expertly around the gorse bushes. Behind them had come others, flowing rapidly down the hill like a flood towards the defenceless group of rabbits. Ernestine had found it hard to drag her eyes away from the two leading creatures. Their pointed ears and sharp-looking teeth fascinated her. The one on the left had blood, presumably Grizz's, smearing its muzzle. The one on the right wore a huge grin, as if it was having the most fun that could be had in the whole world.

Ernestine had sat transfixed, and stared helplessly at her approaching doom. Rabbits called this paralysis the *Gate of Death* – the sheer inability to move that afflicts a rabbit so terrified that it cannot make its muscles work, even to save its life. Humans call it being *scared stiff*. It did not happen to all rabbits, but it was very common. Ernestine's state of *Gate of Death* would quickly lead to her real death if she didn't receive help.

Cuetip had tried to rouse her, but all he could manage was a stuttering "Er- Er- Er". Hobb had penetrated her stupor, though. He had shouted her name, butted her with his head, asked her what was happening. His urgent words had snapped her out of her trance.

"Foxes, Hobb! Foxes!" she had cried, urgently, "Get everyone inside, quickly!"

"OK!" said Hobb, glad to be given something definite to do. He had sped off, yelling warnings to anyone who could hear, trying to use the sheer power of his voice to urge them to hide, to run, to get to safety.

"Run, Cuetip, run!" Ernestine had screamed at him. He had glanced briefly back at the approaching foxes, and been alarmed by how close they had come. One of the leaders had stopped, and was tearing at something it had pinned to the ground, but the others would be on him in seconds. With no thought of choosing a direction, he had simply taken to his heels in a panic.

     * * *

And now he was struggling for his life. As he wriggled on his back, the fox reached him, eyes glinting in anticipation. Luckily it was moving too fast to stop suddenly, and overshot its helpless prey, growling in annoyance. Cuetip frantically squirmed upright, and spotted an oval of darkness beneath nearby gorse. Salvation!

He forced his aching legs into action once more, twisted and ran for the welcoming hole, as a second fox joined the first in the race to kill him. The brief feeling of relief he had felt at spotting the refuge turned to alarm when he saw how far away the burrow actually was.

He felt the hot ground hitting his complaining paws, and could hear the pounding feet of the foxes as they rapidly closed the gap. His breath burned in his chest as he drove his legs faster, and he imagined that he could feel the hot breath of the fox on his back, its jaws open and ready to drive its sharp teeth into his body. The urge to look back was almost unbearable, but he knew that would only slow him down, and so he sped on as fast as he could, wide-eyed and frantic.

A moan of fear grew in his throat, and he willed himself to even greater speed as he neared the burrow entrance, mercifully dark in the glaring sunshine. He flung himself into the shadow, tumbling gratefully head over heels into the welcoming coolness of the burrow. As he rolled, a backwards glance showed a pair of massive jaws with a set of evil teeth snapping into the burrow entrance. Cuetip scuttled further back to a safe distance, then lay on his side, sucking air into his tortured lungs with mighty gasps, and staring at that snarling muzzle, unable to tear his eyes away, imagining what those glistening teeth could have done to him. He had only just made it to safety, and could only hope that everyone else had been quicker than he had.

Fog opening Chapter

You know how it is. You suddenly realise that you are driving along a road, but you have no idea where this road is, or where you are headed. The last ten miles are a blank and for several seconds you wear a puzzled frown, until light eventually dawns and you realise that you're off to the shop for a pot of green paint. Or, to use paint manufacturer's language, *'Pea Pod'*.

Well, that's how it was with me at first. It was as if I'd just blinked into existence at the wheel of this car, driving along a foggy road winding through some woods. I couldn't remember a thing about the journey I'd taken to get to this point. The car headlights were on, presumably because of the fog, but I had no recollection of actually switching them on. Not that unusual a feeling, really. Plenty of you will have experienced it.

Except that in my case I couldn't remember anything else, either. Oh, it was pretty clear that I remembered how to drive a car, since I was managing to change gear smoothly and avoid smashing into the trees.

There was, however, nothing personal in my head; nothing about *me*. For instance (and it's a pretty big instance), well, who was I? I supposed that I must have a name, but what the hell was it? Racking my brain, I felt like I could *almost* grasp it, but it was just out of reach, like when you can't quite remember the name of that bloke who's always in the background of black and white British films from the Fifties.

I eased off the accelerator as the fog thickened, and the trees thickened too. A road sign loomed out of the fog, warning me that I might encounter some deer at this point in my journey. Now, how did I know what the sign meant if my memory wasn't working? And shouldn't I have 'come to' by now? This sort of thing only lasts a few seconds, doesn't it? I began to feel a bit dizzy, and a seed of fear began to grow.

A slightly paler section of the woods to my left proved to be a break in the trees, and I pulled off the road into the gap; the beginning of a rutted track that wound deeper into the forest. I turned off the engine and headlights. It was very quiet. The fog-shrouded trees that I could see through the windscreen looked pretty spooky, and didn't help to ease my growing fear. I got out of the car, leaned against the hot bonnet and breathed deeply, which at least stopped my head spinning. The air was chilly, and I got the feeling that it was early in the day, soon after dawn perhaps.

Perhaps I'd had some kind of mental stroke or, I don't know, psychological trauma thing. I had absolutely no idea what any of those words meant, which probably indicated that I was not any sort of psychiatrist, but you have to understand that I wasn't exactly *compos mentis* at this point and I was desperately trying to make some sense of what might be happening to me.

I had no idea who I was. I had no idea *where* I was. I was a poor little lamb who had lost his way. Now where the hell had *that* phrase come from? A thought slipped into the side of my mind, and before it could slip out again I clutched at it like a drowning man at a cliché. Maybe I just needed to see something familiar to 'jolt' my memory back into life? Like I said, obviously not a psychiatrist.

So, first things first, I started with me. I was male, and wearing an unremarkable plain dark sweatshirt, unremarkable black trousers and unremarkable black trainers. I briefly regretted that I wasn't dressed a bit more flamboyantly, say in a kilt with a *sgian dubh* down my sock, or in a cool black suit with cool black shades and cool black hair, instead of the wiry stuff that grew wildly about my head. With a little trepidation I checked out my face in the wing mirror. Unremarkable, wouldn't you just know it? I seemed to be middle-aged, in my forties at a guess; reasonably good-looking, dusty brown curly hair beginning to thin. Brown eyes, no scars, no facial hair. There was a little cut just below my right eye. I touched it tentatively—it stung, and a smear of blood stained my finger. A fresh cut then, but only small. I grinned at my reflection, and was pleased to see that at least I seemed to have a nice friendly smile and all the right teeth.

OK then, pockets. My right trouser pocket contained a five pound note. I thought it interesting that I could recognise the woman wearing the crown as the queen, although this was not immediately helpful as the fiver failed to provide her telephone number. I became distracted for a while trying to figure out why Her Majesty had what appeared to be a snail attached to her left ear, before carrying on with my search.

Left trouser pocket–sod all. Back pocket–wait, here was something. A thin strip of metal, straight but for oddly shaped ends. One end was bent over a bit, and the other was the shape of a tiny triangular flag. An earwax remover?

Medical probe? Or maybe just a part of something bigger? This was not going very well, I had to admit. So far I had discovered that I looked boring and ordinary, had five quid, collected earwax removers and didn't wear a kilt. Great.

Sam Kydd! That was his name! You know him, that character actor that I was talking about. Sam Kydd. He was never the star, but he was in hundreds of films and television programmes in the Forties, Fifties and Sixties. He was in *The Cruel Sea*, and that Peter Sellers film, what was it–*I'm Alright Jack*.

This brought me up short. How come I knew so much about Sam Kydd, but nothing about myself? Unless *I* was Sam Kydd, of course, but that didn't seem very likely given that he would be well into his nineties by now.

I dragged my thoughts back to the matter in hand. This selective nature of my amnesia had me puzzled. I wondered how I could remember stuff such as driving and Elizabeth the Second and Sam Kydd, but not other, more important things such as who I was, or, say, whether I was married. I quickly checked my fingers–no rings, which of course told me nothing.

I turned my attention to the car. It was a blue Vauxhall Meriva, a few years old from the wear, and in desperate need of a wash. It had two window stickers. One told me that the owner of the car had been in the AA for ten years, and the other was from Grynigg Farm, which was apparently a Red Kite Feeding Centre.

The tax disc had three months to run. Knowing that at least told me that I was aware of the year. I climbed into the passenger seat. Nothing behind the sun visors. I opened the glove compartment, idly wondering whether there would be any actual gloves inside.

As it happened, there were. I smiled inanely at this as I took out a pair of ordinary grey woollen gloves such as an unremarkable man might wear. The glove compartment also disgorged a box of tissues, a CD of Mozart Violin Sonatas without a case, a CD case of the *Jurassic Park* soundtrack without a CD, and a bag of Maltesers. This last discovery made me realise that I was extremely hungry, so I jabbed the Mozart into the CD player and listened while I polished off the chocolates.

As I wiggled my tongue in the honeycomb, I considered the results of my search for an identity. So far, so bleugh. I turned around. There was nothing on the back seat, and nothing in the door pockets save a small pair of scissors.

I sucked the chocolate off the last Malteser, climbed out again into the fog, and leaving the door open I walked round to the back of the car. The merry notes of the *B flat sonata, K454*, floated out into the murk. I pulled the latch and lifted the rear door, which rose slowly with a reluctant wheezing sound.

I think I said "Jesus" at least three times, and "fuck" a hell of a lot more than that. When people say that you can fall back in surprise, they're not exaggerating, you know. I staggered backwards and fell with an involuntary squeak into some damp ferns. My stomach felt queasy, and the Maltesers threatened to make an unscheduled re-appearance.

I managed to stand, and shakily took a step forward, desperately hoping that my imagination was playing tricks in tandem with my memory. I looked again. It was a young woman. She was naked, arms by her sides, legs curled up, eyes staring blankly out of her head. Unfortunately none of these parts—limbs, body, or head—were joined together.

Cubic Scats sample chapter

The Ghost Chicken of Highgate

A conversation with my daughter prompted me to remember something a once girlfriend had told me when I lived in London – that there was a place in Highgate haunted by a Ghost Chicken. No, really, it turns out it's A Thing.

A quick search led me to mentions of Sir Francis Bacon, so I took down my copy of Aubrey's Brief Lives and found this story of events in April 1626 –

"As he (Sir Francis Bacon) was taking the air in a coach with Dr Witherborne (a physician) towards Highgate, snow lay on the ground, and it came into my lord's thoughts, why flesh might not be preserved in snow, as in salt. They were resolved they would try the experiment presently. They alighted out of the coach, and went into a poor woman's house at the bottom of Highgate Hill, and bought a fowl, and made the woman exenterate it, and then stuffed the body with snow, and my lord did help to do it himself. The snow so chilled him, that he immediately fell so extremely ill, that he could not return to his lodging ... but went to the Earle of Arundel's house at Highgate, where they put him into a

good bed warmed with a pan, but it was a damp bed that had not been layn-in about a year before, which gave him such a cold that in two or three days, as I remember Mr Hobbes told me, he died of Suffocation."

Many doubt that Bacon *did* experiment in frozen foods, but people began to report strange happenings, and there were several reported sightings of a particularly eerie apparition around Pond Square from the 17th Century onwards. Yes, the Ghost Chicken was on the loose.

In the second World War the unnerving apparition of a ghost chicken was seen many times. In 1943, Aircraftsman Terence Long was in Pond Square one night when he heard horses' hooves, wheels, and a screeching noise. Instead of a horse and cart though, what he saw when he turned was a half-plucked chicken, flapping its wings and legging it wildly around in a circle before vanishing.

Later, ARP Wardens saw the ghost several times around Pond Square. One tried to bag the incorporeal bird, but failed when it "vanished through a brick wall"

A resident of Pond Square, a Mrs. Greenhill, said after the war that she had seen the ghost, and described it as *"a big, whitish bird"*.

In January 1969, a "large white half-plucked bird" was seen by a driver whose car had broken down. He moved towards it, but it disappeared.

In February 1970 a courting couple were surprised when a ghostly chicken landed beside them, ran round twice, then vanished into thin air. Coitus henterruptus (sorry).

I couldn't find anything after that, so perhaps the pecky phantom has found peace at last.

1322 Preview

WARNING! ADULT CONTENT – if you're not a fan of sexy scenes, you might want to avoid reading the brief first chapter of this sample and skip right to Chapter Two.

1322 will be my next full-length novel, and is loosely based on a real-life event that happened near Northampton in March of that year. It concerns the adventures of a poor minstrel struggling to make his way in a hard world.

A unearthly event at his wife's funeral sets him on a path through 14th Century life which leads him to adventure, humour, shape-shifting, horror, a tantalising mystery, sex, more action than he'd like, a one-eyed mistress of fire, bizarre happenings, a fight in a cabbage patch and a whole heap of fascinating and minutely-researched 14th century detail.

Spiced throughout with medieval song and verse, *1322* should (barring unforeseen impediment) be published around Christmas 2013.

This sample is not final draft, so there are likely to be changes when the novel finally goes to press. Also I've included abbreviated author's notes at the end to explain a little of the Medieval background to the story. Now read on.

1322

A preview of his forthcoming novel
from Michael Wombat
In which readers are cautioned to prepare themselves to read descriptions of the acts of fornication.

1

As I lay upon a nyght for soth y sawe a semely syght

Dark of hair she was and dark of eye, her gaze the depth of a star-spattered night. She peered up at John from beneath lowered brows, and crawled up his naked body. Her full breasts brushed his thighs, teasing upwards as she moved her weight from arm to arm, advancing along his prone nakedness.

Her eyes never left his as she paused her progress along the expanse of his skin. John was unable to move. He felt captive, held by her glittering eyes as a moth beguiled by a bright flame.

The woman continued to sway leisurely from side to side, the warmth of her cleavage nudging his swelling tarse to follow her rhythm.

"You must warm my womb, man," the woman whispered, looking directly into his soul. Glory be to God, but she was beautiful.

No, no, this was wrong. This was not who he was. Who was this woman? This predatory, arousing woman? He knew no women like this. He... he was married. He was wed to

Wynifreed. This female was not his Wyni. Wyni was skinny and bony, a result of growing up through the Great Famine, and had small, boyish breasts and thin, short brown hair.

The woman atop him, oh, this woman was endowed with a roundness that John had rarely seen. The full curve of her buttocks rose behind her. The dance of her breasts bestowed life on his pintle, lifting it from its resting place on his thigh.

And her hair. Her hair was a deep black-blue, the colour of a raven's feather, falling luxuriously to frame her slightly amused face, a stray lock only enhancing the beauty of her face. The strange woman's eyes sparkled and she smiled as she began to move back and forth, bringing his tarse to full alertness.

John whimpered and watched the slow, erotic movements of the woman's body. Wyni had never moved like this.

Had never? Wait, there was something he was forgetting. Something important. Something about Wyni. What was it now? He flicked his eyes to one side and tried to think.

The woman frowned, and moved all her weight onto her left arm. She licked her right forefinger sensually, her tongue flicking from between full lips. She ran the wet tip of her finger along the length of him, once, twice. He felt his seed stir deep within. Her eyes captured his gaze once more.

Where were they? John could no longer tear his look away from hers, but his brief sideways glance had shown him the branches of a huge tree, spreading above them.

Beyond this he got the impression of a dark purple sky paling to violet. They were definitely not in his house with its thatched roof, not in his little toft. Not where he had fallen asleep.

The strange female crept further up his body, still locking his gaze with her bewitching eyes. She lowered her head to drag her tongue slowly across his chest. He watched her great dark wings unfold above and around him, like a cocoon.

He felt her pubic hair against his genitals, brushing the excited flesh with the lightest of touches. Her tempting mouth neared his, but she raised her head tantalisingly away from his hungry lips. Her breath smelled of fennel.

She stretched her nakedness along his body, thigh to thigh, belly to belly, chest to chest. Her voluptuous hips rotated against his overexcited groin and she bent her lovely mouth to his ear. She licked it wetly and warmly as he felt his seed begin to rise urgently.

"Follow the owl. Find me," she whispered, and vanished.

2

Of al this world ne give I it a pese

John cried out as he woke. His belly was wet, the hair of his chest sticky and matted.

"Clotpole!" he cursed, "Eating too much lettuce, John."

He looked about him, bleary-eyed. Dimly he could make out a thatched roof, lime-washed cob walls, and the embers of last night's fire. He was in his own house, prone on a pallet on his own floor.

A chill breeze forced its way through the narrow shuttered windows, causing John to shiver. What had possessed him to throw off his blankets on a cold night?

That dream, that's what. It had felt so real. He looked down at his disappearing erection and shivered again. He rolled from the pallet and grabbed a rag to wipe the stickiness from his body.

Shaking from the cold, he stepped over Ailred's sleeping bulk, opened the door and looked up. The pre-dawn sky was a dull peach colour in the east, but overhead the stars still flickered. He reached down and took a faggot from the wood piled by the door.

Back inside he threw the log on the remains of last night's fire and fanned the glow with the rag. When he was sure that the flame was established, he dragged his rough mattress closer to the warmth and lay back down, pulling the blankets around him.

Ailred muttered in his sleep before settling into a deep harmonious snore. It would take a lot to wake him after last night's excesses. By God, the man could drink.

John stared at the curling flames as they grew, warming the chilly room and the backs of his companions. They had made a fine wake, dancing and singing until the small hours, recounting tales of Wyni's joyful laughter, her love of life and nature. She would have enjoyed it immensely, had she been present in more than just body.

Shame, deep shame gripped him and he screwed up his eyes, as if to banish the guilt from his mind. It refused to budge. He had betrayed Wyni. Betrayed her in the worst way a man could, in his dreams. How could he dream of swiving another woman on the eve of his wife's funeral? How he regretted his half-awake quip about the effects of lettuce.

He thought of Wyni, her infectious laugh lost to him now. He remembered how beautiful she had looked the day that they had wed, a circlet of daisies about her brown head, her smile dazzling in the sunshine. When she had revealed her slim figure to him that night, he had thought he'd never seen anything so beautiful.

A curve of the flame around the wood pulled his thoughts back to the woman in his dream, and the way she had moved her full breasts against him. His hand snaked down between his legs.

"No!" he hissed, and withdrew his fingers.

"What?" piped a voice from the far side of the fire, beyond the snoring Ailred.

"Sorry, nothing," John said, quietly, "Return to sleep, Ralf."

"Tempting, but I'm about to burst. I need a piss."

"Well, don't do it on my herb garden like last time. Use the privy, you filthy sod."

"Nag, nag, nag," countered Ralf, rising to his feet with a wobble. "You should put your privy nearer the door if you don't want pissed-upon thyme."

He was a tall man with a shock of red hair, and still fully dressed from the night before. He stretched his long legs over the considerable mound of Ailred, and went outside. Moments later, John heard a stream of liquid hitting the cobbles just outside the window.

"Oi!" he shouted, "Away from the house too, you pisspot!" He was rewarded with laughter from outside.

"Hens!" shouted Ailred, waking suddenly. He sat up and looked around with a startled expression, resembling a bewildered owl in the orange light thrown up by the now merrily burning fire. Smoke curled up into the blackness of the roof.

Ailred scratched his beard, dislodging a small bone, which he inspected closely. He descended into a fit of deep coughing. Eventually he achieved some sort of resolution with his lungs and spat copiously in the fire, which hissed a complaint. He threw the bone into the flames.

"What hour?" rumbled the burly smith, "Is the house awake?"

"Almost dawn," replied John, "We have no hurry. We can spend most of prime preparing ourselves before the procession."

"Good. God's teeth, my back aches. I am glad that Wyni was but a slight figure, for I doubt that I am up to much carrying. I blame that ridiculous dance with... what's her name? The scary widow; the one with odd teeth who laid Wyni out? She never shuts up."

"Rohesia," John answered, and a smirk appeared on his lips. "You know she's looking for another husband, don't you? A smith, probably."

"That's disturbing," grated the big man, "I'd better make shift before my thoughts dwell too much on *those* possibilties."

"Yes, move your fat arse!" declared Ralf, striding back inside and aiming a kick at his friend's backside. "Coming on to rain, John."

"Arse," cursed John. Just what they needed, a slippery road and a slippery bier to carry. Still, there was nothing to be done about that. He took a deep breath against the cold and threw off his blankets again. He stood and stretched in the dawning light.

"Oh, may it please both God and all his angels, cover yourself up, man," complained Ralf. "The last thing I want to see of a morning is your withered acorn."

John grinned and threw on his clothes. He poured himself a mug of water to rinse out his mouth, spitting out of the window. He chewed a few dried herbs from a small bowl on the table.

"Wake the good baker," he told the others, and picked up his gittern and a quill. He plucked experimentally at the strings, pleased that it had held its tone through the cold night. While Ralf and Ailred merrily flicked water and small twigs at the yet slumbering fourth member of their vigil, John tried to think of a respectful rhyme for 'Wyni'.

His wife's soul would be in purgatory now, paying for the few sins she had committed in her life, and they were few indeed. She had been a loving, kind woman whom John had, although never consumed by uncontrollable passion, always loved and cared for. A good song in her praise would help her neighbours and friends remember to pray for her through the month's mind, and speed her passage through the torment of Purgatory to heaven.

'*Skinny*'? No, no, he must put his jester hat to one side for this song. He needed to be a true minstrel. '*Destiny*' perhaps? Yes, yes, that would work.

"My good lady Wyni," he tried, "As the goddess Athene. Was... erm, was took by destiny... curse it, that's not good."

As John worked on his song, his other three vigilants prepared themselves for the funeral. Ralf and Ailred finally succeeded in waking Pentecost, the village baker, a lithe and lively man who obviously did not overeat on his loaves and buns. After all, they were his living. As he had often said, "I prefer greatly to sell bread than to eat it. Rather give me eels and fish any day."

"Did Wyni like horses?" asked Ralf, rummaging about on the floor for his shoes.

"No," answered John, "Why?"

"Whinny," explained the tall gongfermour, "*'My good lady Wyni like a horse she would whinny'*. Perfect rhyme."

"Be still, gabbler. Your wit has as much joy and delight as your work."

"Someone has to move all the shit," said Ralf, "Lest my Lord happen to see any when he ventures out here. Speaking of which, are you working tonight?"

"As far as I know I am not, thanks to God. I do not imagine that I will feel very entertaining after the funeral."

A deep bell rang once a short distance away.

"St. Giles calls for us, my worthies!" bellowed Ailred, handing over a small black cloth. John put down his instrument and tied the cloth around his left arm. Then he joined the other three in walking through to the back room. There in the gloom lay Wyni's corpse, wrapped in a winding sheet and resting on the parish bier. The men positioned themselves at the four corners.

"Ready?" asked John. His companions nodded. They lifted the bier and walked slowly outside, each gripping a handle at the corner of the stretcher.

A chill drizzle hit John's face as he emerged into the pale light of the grey morning. Perfect. That would suit his mood just right. While Wyni had been in the bedroom at home he had felt fine, but now that her corpse was about to be interred he began to feel a growing sense of loss and sadness.

The four men left John's toft with their burden and turned along the muddy lane towards the church of St. Giles.

The dismal weather began to affect John's mood. The bell of St. Giles sounded again, a single low, lingering lament.

As they moved carefully along, the sexton, a bald little man named Pons, hurried up to them from the direction of the church. As he neared he shrugged at John and shook his head. He had been unable to find the parish handbell, normally used to proceed funeral processions. The church bell alone would have to suffice to protect Wnyi's soul from any hungry demons lurking in the murky air.

The sexton would be in big trouble for losing the bell, not only with Father Ilbert but also, if it was not found, with the manor lord. The sexton took his place at the head of their little procession anyway, but without a bell to ring he looked a bit lost, like a dog without its owner.

The drizzle worsened. As the water drenched him, and began to drip from the end of his nose, John considered his reactions to his wife's murder.

He had been horrified at the act that had ended her life, but was sanguine about the fact that she was dead. Death was a normal part of life, reached by all. Wyni had lived longer on the Lord's earth than many others, and had enjoyed her time here. He hoped that she would not linger long in Purgatory, God have mercy, for she had been a good woman.

Well, mostly. She had giggled in church that one time during service, interrupting the priest in his solemn reading. That had been John's fault, though, for farting after too much cabbage soup the previous night. Perhaps God would realise that.

John smiled, and was thankful that he was leading the procession so that none could see his inappropriate mirth. Wyni's giggle had been infectious, and they had both been stifling helpless laughter by the end of the service. That night they had made happy love, the last time that their bodies had come together.

Three days later Wyni's corpse was found half-naked in a ditch. She had been visiting her cousin, who was with child, over in Courteenhall. She had set off for the three mile journey home at mid-day. When she did not return home by dusk, John had worried, but thought that perhaps she had decided to stay away an extra night.

The following morning, the priest had knocked at his door. Somehow he knew immediately that she was lost to him. Priests do not routinely visit the houses of minstrels, particularly not priests as strait-laced as Father Ilbert.

The father had sat him down, and told him the details. A tinker had spotted Wyni's body in the ditch by the side of the road. She was naked from the waist down. Her thighs were badly bruised. She had been cut about the face with a sharp knife, and her throat slit. There had been... other signs that Wyni had been violated sexually. Father Ilbert had been reluctant to share those details, and John had had no desire to find out any more.

Villagers slowly emerged from their houses and followed behind, maintaining a respectful silence. Many wore black cloths around their arm, while a few wore full mourning – a simple black dress, or a black cloak with a white lining. John was pleased to see that Wyni would receive the prayers of some of the more well-to-do villagers. Both men and women wore hats or drew up their hoods against the weather. All became sodden in seconds as the drizzle strengthened into a proper downpour. The heavy rain soaked the winding sheet tightly wrapped around Wyni's body, and spattered against the cloth that covered her face as if the veil of anonymity had already fallen.

After Father Ilbert had left, John had wept for a time, with great racking sobs and snot-dripping nose. Then anger had grown out of grief and he had cursed and roared. He had sworn bloody revenge against those who had taken Wyni's life. Except that there were no clues as to who that had been, other than that there had been more than a single attacker.

Tears welled into his eyes again, and John was grateful now for the rain, which would hide the tears. He gave a great sniff. Ralf, alongside him at the front of the bier, gave a sideways glance.

"Steady, John," he said quietly. Perhaps the rain wasn't as good a disguise as he'd thought.

By God, but his moods had been swinging wildly these last two days. Fury gave way to grief, to horror, and then just as quickly to acceptance and, occasionally, laughter. Father Ilbert told him that this was a good thing – that too much grief might imply a lack of faith in the deceased's salvation.

After all, Wyni was now on her journey to bathe in the wonder of God, and who would doubt that that was a wonderful thing? He would rather that her portal to heaven had been more easily opened, however.

The four men splashed through noisome mud now, their boots disturbing the filth, sticks, rotting leaves, small bones, all the detritus of village life. Hens clattered away from their feet as they plodded along. Just a few more yards and they would be at the church.

John struggled to remember Wyni's final words to him. He could remember her penultimate words to him clearly and perfectly: "Practice while I am gone, John! You do not want to disappoint with your performance tonight!" Always with the nagging, always wanting him to get in the Baron's good books, starting with his reeve in this village. True, the Baron already had a chief minstrel in his retinue, a Frenchman named Jaufre, but there was always room for more, to cover for sickness, to play at minor events that the Baron himself did not attend.

Wyni was tired of her husband's long absences, as he travelled miles from fair to market to fair for the sake of a few shillings. The travelling would lessen greatly if he could only be accepted into the Baron's service. Wyni had helped his music a lot, with her pushing and prompting and, admit it John, her help with setting the songs. Now she had wanted to help his career, too.

He could not bring to mind her exact parting words, however. It had been a form of farewell as she left for Courteenhall, basket in hand, but as to the exact words? They were a mystery to him now.

He flicked his head to throw water from his brow, and passed his free hand across his head to squeeze it out of his thick blonde hair. The bier wobbled as behind him one of the rear two slipped on the slimy ordure beneath their feet before righting themselves. They must clean their feet well once they reached the church porch. John hoped that Father Ilbert had made plenty of cloths ready for the task.

The procession turned right and entered the churchyard gate, a simple gap in the low stone wall that surrounded the church land. The rain slashed into their faces. They walked on cobbles now, laid last year to provide the church with a proper path. The path took them between the graves of the wealthy dead, mostly high officials who had paid the church good money for a prime position. The highest of the high, of course, would be in the church itself. John read one of the markers as they passed:

Here lieth under this grave Riche Alan, the bald man; God give his soul peace.

Such an exalted position did not await Wyni's remains. She was just a minstrel's wife, and John had little money with which to pay for such a plot.

No, Wyni would be buried in the communal area of the churchyard, around the back. At least she would lay in consecrated ground, and as memory of her subsided, so her body would decay into the earth, joining the group of Christian souls that lay there, until eventually they were disinterred and integrated into the charnels under the church eaves.

Or rather, John corrected himself, the Christian bodies would be disinterred. The souls of the dead would be on their way to heaven, via the torments of Purgatory.

Father Ilbert awaited them, dry in the cover of the porch. He was wearing his ceremonial cope, and he was frowning. The procession paused in the small church entrance. John bowed his head, and smiled, but the priest's stern expression did not waver.

"Thank you for this, Father," John said, "I know it was not an easy decision for you."

He cast his mind back to their meeting of the previous day, when the Father had called to discuss the arrangements for the funeral.

"John, you must know that I loved your wife. She was a strength to the church, and her assistance with the cleaning and the flowers will be rewarded in Heaven. However..."

Father Ilbert had paused and looked uncomfortably at his feet.

"What?" John had asked, "However what?" The priest had sighed.

"However," he had continued, "I cannot allow Wyni's remains to enter the church building. You will have to take her directly to the grave."

"You ca... what? Why in God's name not?"

"In God's name indeed – and it is due to the manner of her ending. I am sorry about this, but—"

"Are you serious? I apologise, Father, but you cannot deny my Wyni, my good Wyni who was always respectful of God's law, you cannot deny her the assistance of God's grace through Purgatory."

"John, listen—"

"No *you* listen," John had spat, his voice rising, "She helped you! She always helped at the church. You will NOT deny her this!"

"The body of a person who has died violently cannot be borne into the church lest the pavement become polluted with blood!" Father Ilbert had barked. John had jumped to his feet.

"I care not a fart of my arse for your pavement; you should be concerning yourself with Wyni. She assisted you for years, and now you have to assist her on her final journey!"

John had collapsed back onto his stool, all his strength gone.

"You just have to," he sobbed. He put his head in his hands. Father Ilbert laid a consoling hand on his shoulder.

"Be still, John," the priest said, more calmly. "Perhaps you have a point. Perhaps... perhaps I can make an exception for Wyni, given all the time that she gave to God."

"Please," John had pleaded, peering through his tears at the priest. Father Ilbert had sighed deeply, and leaned back in his chair.

"Do you have any ale?" he had asked, surprisingly.

"Erm, yes."

"Then for the Lord's sake, get me an ale and Wyni can lie in the nave overnight. Do not expect me to be cheerful about it, however."

A wave of relief had washed over John, and he had shared his last jug of ale with the priest. He dragged his mind back to the present.

John, Ralf, Ailred and Pentecost wiped their feet thoroughly on the rushes laid down on the floor and the cloths that Pons handed them. Father Ilbert gestured for them to follow, and they bore their burden a few yards into the church itself, then laid it down on its short feet beside the hearse, the metal framework which would be set over the body.

The men stretched and rubbed their aching arms. Rainwater dripped from the bier onto the church floor. John looked nervously, but thankfully the drips remained clear.

The hearse was covered with the Parish pall, a black and gold hearse-cloth made of Italian velvet, donated by a widow from the few rich houses at the upper end of the village. On it, picked out in gold thread, were the words "*Orate pro animabus Henrici Chester et Aliciae uxoris eius*" – "Pray for the souls of Henry Chester and his wife Alice." The widow Alice, with such a gift, had ensured that her late husband, and eventually herself, would benefit from the prayers of everyone in the parish at every funeral held there.

There was little light inside the church on this gloomy day, but once all the mourners had filed in, enough daylight managed to struggle through the open doors and the small windows so that Father Ilbert decided to forego lighting candles that were better saved until later.

The villagers mostly sat down in the pews, nodding at John as they passed. A few reached out to him, and gave a soft word of condolence. Rohesia, the widow, entered, giving Ailred a sly wink as she passed. The smith's chin tensed.

John and the other three bearers stood by the bier. Father Ilbert sprinkled the body with blest water & incense, and commenced a short welcoming speech of his own devising. He had found that his flock the better observed the proper rituals if first they were bound to the services by a few personalised words about the deceased.

"The proper liturgies will of course be observed later, but may it please you now to pray for the soul of our departed Wynifreed. Remember her and ease her suffering. She was known to us all here, and friend we called her. She cleaned this, our church. She made many of the clothes that now you wear. The village is the poorer for her departure into the next world. Glory be to God."

"Thank you," John mouthed to the priest.

"The Office of the Dead will commence this day at evensong, and Wynifreed's earthly remains will be interred after the Dirige tomorrow morning. Let those now present observe silence for a time, while we consider the departed and pray for her soul."

Silence fell in the dimly-lit church, save for the hiss of the rain lashing down outside. Many heads were bowed, but John looked about him. He would spend much of his life on thoughts of his wife, and it would not hurt to examine his surroundings so that he could retain this moment as more than a fragment of memory.

Deep shadows were cast across the alcoves at the each side of the nave. Father Ilbert bowed his head, dressed in his finery. The air smelled cool and fragrant.

A voice skimmed the silence. A woman's voice, singing sweetly a song that John quickly realised that he knew.

Wanne mine ehnen misten
And mine heren sisses
And mine nosen coldet
And mine tunge foldet

Heads lifted and looked to the doorway, from where the song drifted. No-one was visible, only the rain pounding down on the churchyard outside, tight hard squally showers that drifted erratically across the entrance. The voice continued, lilting and ethereal.

> *And mine rude slaket*
> *And mine lippes blaken*
> *And my muth grenet*
> *And my spotel rennet*

Father Ilbert's face twisted into an expression of outrage. He took a stride forward and raised his voice.

"Break not God's silence! You cannot—"

The unseen singer took not a jot of notice. The rain eased a little.

> *And my her risset*
> *And my herte grisset*
> *And mine hinden bivien*
> *And mine fet stivien*

The priest clenched his fists and made to march toward the door. John held up a hand to stay him. The rain lessened further to a light drizzle, now lit brightly from the side as the sun emerged. The doorway took on an otherworldly quality, dark brooding skies now a backdrop to a glowing rainbow mist across the portal.

> *Al to late, al to late*

"Aaaah!" a woman exclaimed loudly. All eyes turned to Rohesia. She was pointing at Wyni's body, wrapped tightly in its soggy winding sheet. A dark stain had appeared at the throat. As John watched the mark spread, seeping into the linen and spreading slowly, a deep scarlet oozing out of the corpse.

The onlookers watched, horrified yet hypnotised, as a second mark appeared between Wyni's legs, and also began to spread, bleeding into the cloth. The unseen woman's lament continued to echo hauntingly around the walls.

Thane I schel flutte
From bedde to flora
From flora to here
From here to bere
From bere to putte
And te putte fordet

John turned back to the doorway, startled now to see a figure, hooded and cloaked, silhouetted against the eerie glow. Sparkling light shone around the form, seeming almost to emanate from it. The figure lifted its cloak away from its body, so that it looked all the world like wings being readied for flight.

"An angel!" whispered Pentecost, crossing himself.

The mourners in the pews gasped, several of them falling to their knees, as the word was passed from mouth to mouth.

"An angel!"

Almost without thinking, John found his lips moving, joining in with the dying lines of the song.

Al to late, al to late
Thane lyd minehus uppe mine nose
Of al this world ne give I it a pese

1322 is expected
towards the end of 2014

1322 preview notes

Chapter 1

Tarse – penis. It was well-used in a late 15th century ballad – *"Now ye speke of a tarse! In all the warld is not a warse, than hathe my hosbond"*. In the 14th century none of the words we use nowadays for that part of the anatomy were in use. 'Tarse' is the oldest such word in English, first appearing in an 11th century book on wort-cunning (the medicinal use of worts and herbs). Other early words are 'ware' and 'pintle'. Both of those appear in a ballad called *"A Talk of Ten Wives on Their Husband's Ware"*. One wife complains *"Owre syre breche when hit is torn, hys pintle pepyth owte beforn lyke a warbrede"*. In other words, her husband's 'pintle' was like a mere worm. The word 'penis' is not known before the 16th century.

Warm my womb – this phrase originates in medieval medical beliefs, which were very much based on the teachings of the third-century writer Galen. He held that women's wombs are 'cold' and need constant warming by 'hot' male sperm. In addition, if women do not regularly copulate their 'seed' might coagulate and suffocate their wombs, damaging their health. Yes, he was a big old perv, but his ideas were taken as read in the Middle Ages.

Chapter 2

Lettuce was thought to *"multiplieth milk in wommen and semen in men"* ("On The Properties Of Things")

Gittern – a relatively small, quill-plucked, gut strung instrument that originated around the 13th century.

Toft – the area upon which a villager's house is built. The 'yard', if you will.

Gongfermour – someone whose job it was to dig out and removed human excrement from privies and cesspits.

Printed in Great Britain
by Amazon